Jack and Annie's Story Word Book

To Kaitlin on her 3rd Birthday
Love Auntie Anne & Uncle George

For Clementine and Conrad

KINGFISHER
a Houghton Mifflin Company imprint
215 Park Avenue South, New York, New York 10003
www.houghtonmifflinbooks.com

First published in 2002
10 9 8 7 6 5 4 3 2 1

Copyright © Rebecca Elgar 2002

LIBRARY OF CONGRESS CATALOGING-IN-PUBLICATION DATA has been applied for.

ISBN 0-7534-5560-9

Printed in China
1TR/0602/TIMS/FR(FR)115OGPR

Jack and Annie's Story Word Book

Rebecca Elgar

KINGFISHER

NEW YORK

house

tree

hedge

Here is Jack's house.
Jack lives at number three.

Hello, Jack. It's time to get up.

roof

window

fence

door

flowers

1

**Here is Annie's house.
Annie lives at number one.**

Hello, Annie. It's time to get up.

Jack is in his bathroom.

"Washing my face," says Jack.

bubble bath

pink washcloth

hairbrush

toy duck

red toothbrush

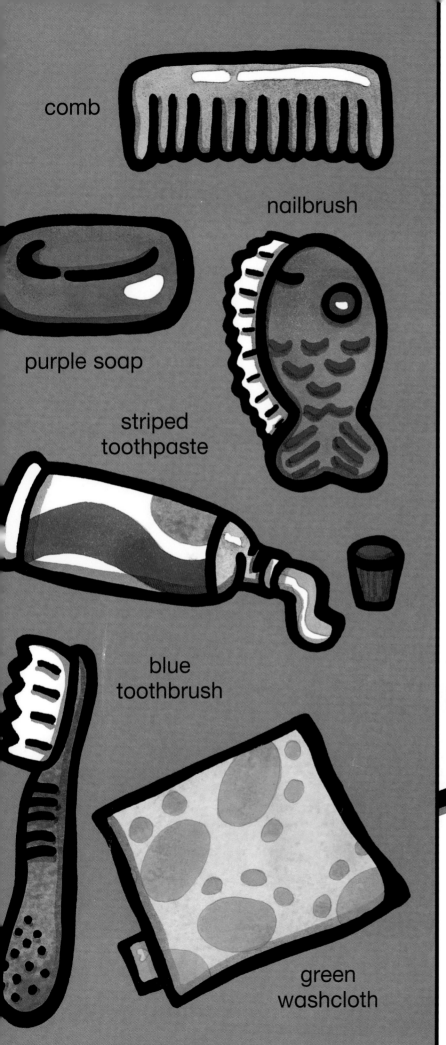

comb

nailbrush

purple soap

striped
toothpaste

blue
toothbrush

green
washcloth

Annie is
in her
bathroom.

"Brushing
my teeth,"
says Annie.

Annie is getting dressed. What would you like to wear today?

"My favorite pink dress," says Annie.

pink dress

hiking boots

fluffy sweater

frilly socks

muddy
overalls

flowered
shirt

sneakers

fancy dress

swimsuit

jeans

flowered shorts

polka-dot pajamas

Jack is getting dressed. What would you like to wear today?

"My new red T-shirt," says Jack.

blue shirt

red T-shirt

striped sneakers

odd socks

shorts

checkered pajamas

star sweater

jeans

white socks

blue
sweatpants

hooded coat

green T-shirt

orange
sandals

It's breakfast time.
Jack is having cereal and toast.

"With peanut butter, please," says Jack.

peanut butter

muffin

banana

milk

strawberry jelly

yogurt

spoon

cereal

bowl

plate

toast

Annie is
having yogurt
and a banana.

"And a muffin,
please,"
says Annie.

Annie is going to nursery school in her stroller.

"Through the park," says Annie.

duck

kite

fluffy dog

butterfly

prickly
leaf

high slide

spotted
dog

little blue
flower

seesaw

teensy-weensy
bug

Jack is riding his scooter to nursery school.

"Look at the yellow loader!" says Jack.

fast black motorcycle

pickup truck

orange bus

slow green
tractor

blue crane

bicycle

noisy
yellow
loader

Annie is already
at nursery school.
Can you see
her coat?
Now hang your
coat up, Jack.

"On my own hook,"
says Jack.

DAN

ROSIE

LUCY

GEORGE

CLEMENTINE

MAGGIE

JACK

JOSH

ANNIE

TIM

Annie is playing in the music corner.

"With my big drum!" shouts Annie.

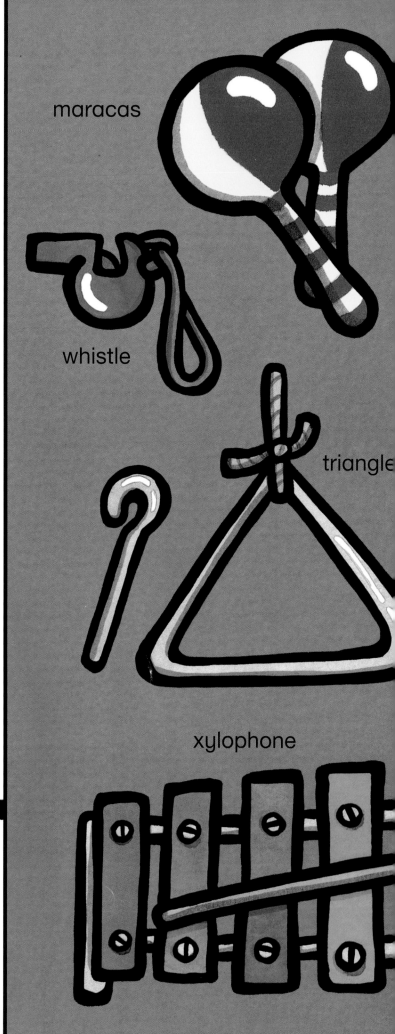

maracas

whistle

triangle

xylophone

drum

tambourine

trumpet

bells

recorder

Jack is painting a picture.

"I need lots of colors," says Jack.

green paint

glue

big paintbrush

red paint

sticky shapes

construction paper

small paintbrush

pink glitter

yellow paint

crayons

blue paint

Time for lunch, everyone.

sandwiches

apple slices

orange juice

raisins

glass of milk

potato chips

cherry yogurt

Wash your hands first.

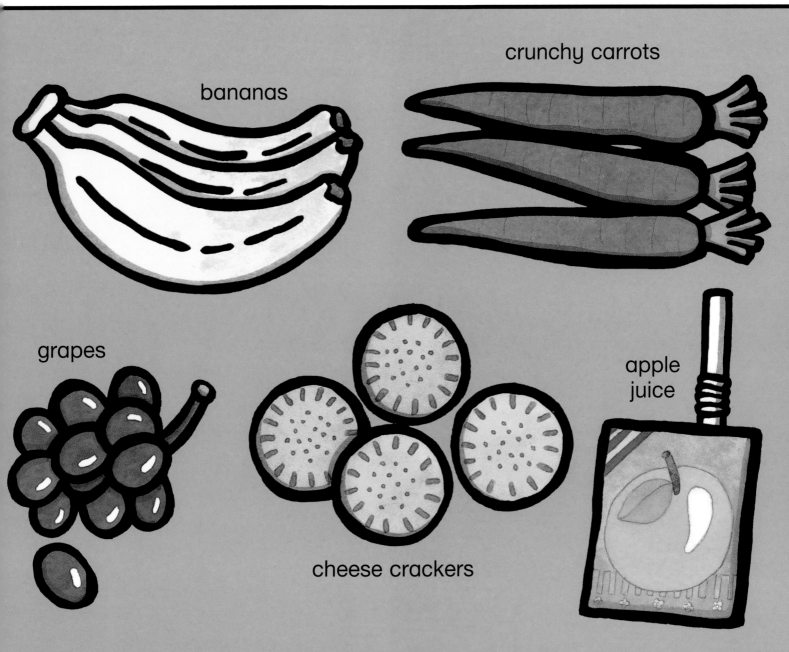

bananas

crunchy carrots

grapes

cheese crackers

apple juice

Now let's play dress-up. Is there a hat for everyone?

pirate hat

straw hat

crown

baseball hat

clown hat

cowboy hat

chef's hat

woolen hat

flowery hat

hard hat

Where would you like to play next?

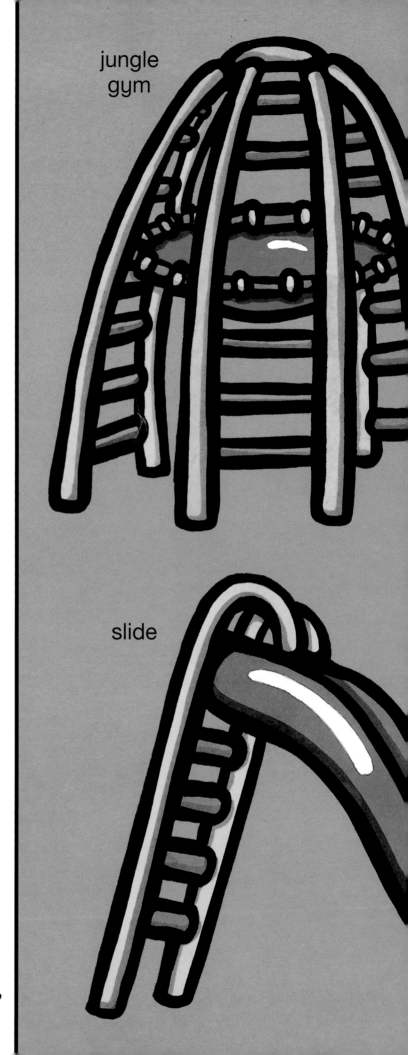

jungle gym

slide

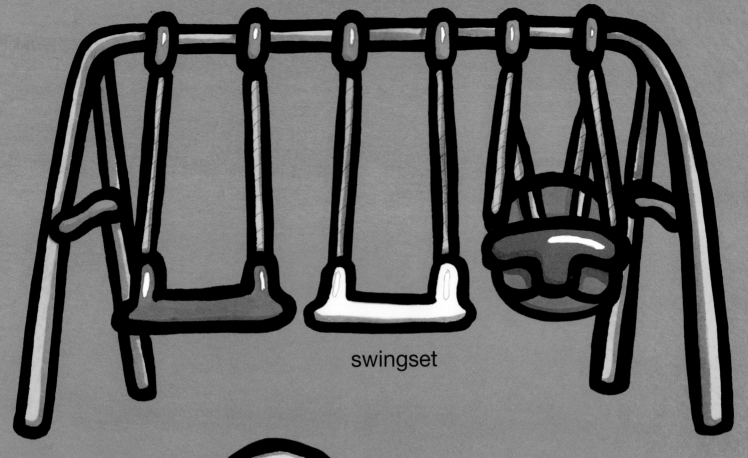

swingset

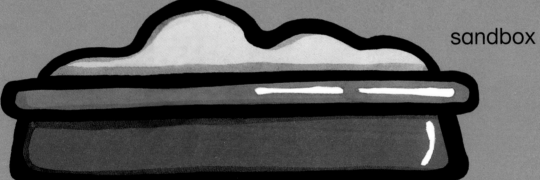

sandbox

playhouse

"I want to play in the sandbox," says Jack.

"With the red pail for making castles."

blue ball

brown teddy bear

orange boat

red
pail

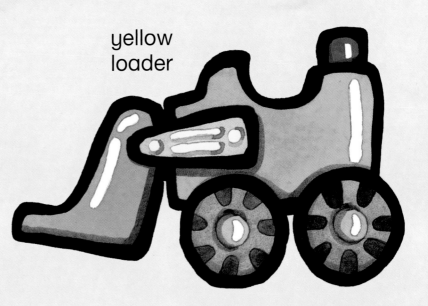

yellow
loader

doll

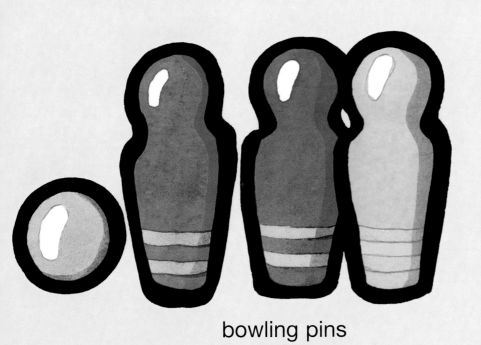

bowling pins

green train

"I want to play in the sandbox," says Annie.

"With the green shovel for digging."

race car

green shovel

jigsaw puzzle

book

toy farm

jump
rope

blue airplane

musical phone

Jack and Annie play together.

They are best friends.

Note to parents

Sharing a good book with young children is an ideal way to help them develop the skills they will need to learn to read. This colorful word book tells the engaging story of best friends Jack and Annie. As you read the story try using different voices for Annie and Jack so that your child can identify more closely with the characters—your child will love this!

Each page features everyday objects in a familiar setting— the home, the park, and nursery school. Name the objects on the page, pointing to the words as you do so. This will help your child understand that spoken words have a written equivalent. Soon your child will join in, pointing to and naming some, and then all, of the objects independently.

Toddlers will also enjoy talking about the story and the pictures and describing their own preferences: what they like for breakfast, what they would choose to wear, how they get to nursery school.

On the opposite page you will find some suggestions for simple games to play to further develop your child's observational and verbal skills.

This book can be enjoyed by children of different ages and abilities, so always go at your child's pace, and offer plenty of praise and encouragement along the way.

Have fun learning about words!

Games to play

I spy

This is a game that all children love. Encourage your child to point to and name specific objects. For example, *I spy with my little eye something you can put on your feet . . . Yes, sneakers / frilly socks!*

Letter sounds

Ask your child to listen for words beginning with a particular letter or letter sound. *Can you find something beginning with "b" (or "buh")? . . . Yes, a banana!*

Colors

Jack's painting page is a great starting point for looking at colors. *What can you see that's blue? . . . Yes, the blue paint / sticky shape / crayon.* You can also look for colors on the other pages: the blue bubble bath / toothbrush / jeans / little blue flower.

Shapes and patterns

Help your child look for simple shapes, such as round shapes or circles: buttons / wheels / cheese crackers / balls. You could also look for patterns, such as checks and stripes.

Matching

Throughout the book, there are opportunities to match items from the story with the labeled objects. For example, in the bathroom: *Can you find Jack's washcloth? Who do you think might use the other washcloth?* When Annie is getting dressed, help your child look for a top to match her flowered shorts.

Numbers and counting

Counting and recognizing the numbers 1 to 10 is an important skill. You can ask your child to count specific objects, such as the socks on Jack's clothes page or the bowling pins on the toy page. And there are ten characters at nursery school, providing loads of fun opportunities to count and match: ten pictures over ten coat hooks, ten hats on ten little heads.